BLENDED

My Happily Ever After

by Bridgette Halley

To Matt, Vanessa, James, and Morgan:

Our road to becoming a cohesive new family has not been perfect, but I know that we are stronger and better today for every challenge. Thank you for all of the laughs, hugs, tears, memories, and most of all, love.

To Jennifer, Chasity, and Brook:

Thanks for helping me to take the final leap of faith.

For I know the plans I have for you, declares

the LORD, plans to prosper you and not to

harm you, plans to give you hope and a future.

Jeremiah 29:11

CHAPTER ONE

Just the Two of Us

I was only one year old when Mom and Dad divorced. Now that I'm seven and Mom is about to marry Kevin, I can't help but think I'm the reason Mom and Dad divorced. No one has ever said I was the reason, but they had been married several years before I came along. Then suddenly, they stopped getting along. Mom later told me that the divorce had nothing to do with me, but I also couldn't help but think that this might be one of those times your parents avoid telling you the truth just to make you feel better.

Like the time I came in next to last place during the fifty-yard dash. I am (or was) the fastest girl in second grade, only ten seconds behind the fastest boy in the whole grade. I thought I had the race in the bag, and I was determined to get the ribbon to prove it. Mom told me that I got my track skills from her because she loved to run too when she was my age. She even ran track in middle and high school. So when the big day came, Mom was there on the sidelines to cheer me on. And she cheered me on even after I finished in next to last place.

"Honey, you did great. What is important is that you participated and gave it your best," she said.

The truth was that I did not do great. I did not give it my best. I completely lost confidence after other kids began to pass me. I decided I couldn't win and gave up during the race.

Or, it's like when Mom told me that I had to get a shot at the doctor's office.

"The pain of the needle won't last long; you won't feel a thing," she said.

And "Just sit really still sweetheart, it will be over before you know it."

But this is just what parents say to make us a little less upset about getting a shot. We all know how this *really* goes. The needle was in my arm for at least half an hour, AND I sat *really, really* still. The truth is that shots hurt!

So even though Mom says that I did not cause her and dad to get a divorce, there's a tiny part of me that wonders if I can believe her.

After the divorce, Mom and I moved into an apartment to be closer to Mom's new job, and we settled into our new life. Just the two of us. I love looking at all of our old photos together. Mom says that I loved to feed the ducks, and we spent many of our weekends at the park.

I love seeing my early Halloween costumes. I think it's a little ironic that I was a lion for my very first Halloween and then a ladybug the following year. It seems I had an affection for animals and bugs pretty early on.

Mom and I seemed to travel a lot together too. The two of us visited Aunt Sarah in Washington, D.C. Mom said that was my first trip on a plane. I spewed a bottle of milk on the passenger sitting next to us, but Mom said that the passenger was a Mom too and understood. Now Mom says that maybe that flight was an indication that I wouldn't enjoy flying very much because even now, I don't look forward to flying. I always feel a little fearful about the plane crashing.

Mom told me that she always says a prayer before take-off, asking God to protect everyone on the plane and that we arrive at our destination safely. So I started doing this too. It helps.

We also visited MiMi and Grandpa in Alabama. I would spend the plane ride drawing each of them a special picture or reading books with Mom. Grandpa taught me how to put slimy worms on my hook and toss the fishing rod into the Mobile Bay while Mom shared stories of her fishing alongside Grandpa, Aunt Sarah, and Uncle Bo when they were kids.

Mom took *me* trick or treating.

Mom fed ducks with *me*.

Mom cooked meals for *me*.

Mom reads books to *me*.

Mom traveled with *me*.

Mom fished with me.

I knew that Mom loved me, and I loved her. The two of us, as happy as could be.

This I believed.

CHAPTER TWO

The Guest

After the divorce, Mom and I started attending a new church, which eventually brought Kevin into our lives. I was in the kindergarten Sunday school class, while Mom and Kevin were volunteer teachers for the fifth-grade girls' and boys' classes. One Sunday, Kevin invited Mom to dinner with him one evening, just the two of them.

They started going on dates, and Ms. Viola would come over to take care of me and put me to bed.

Mom had never gone on any dates before Kevin. I mean, I'd never had a babysitter to come over in the evenings to watch me. Also, each time Mom announced that Ms. Viola was coming over, she'd get dressed really pretty. Mom usually didn't dress up other than for church, holidays, or a special event like my preschool graduation. And when Kevin rang the doorbell, I noticed she smelled extra sweet as she hugged and kissed me goodbye.

Often I'd let Ms. Viola think I was asleep in bed, but I was only waiting up for Mom to come home. Each time she'd quietly tiptoe in and softly talk to Ms. Viola. Each time I'd hear Mom ask, "So how did Mia do?"

"Easy breezy," Ms. Viola would reply.

After I heard Ms. Viola leave, I'd come out of my bedroom, rubbing my eyes, pretending to have been asleep only to have Mom tuck me back into bed.

I mean, Mom and I had a goodnight routine, and I wanted to stick to it.

Each night, for as long as I can remember, I picked out a book that Mom would read aloud to me and crawled into bed. Then I'd say my prayer, and Mom said a prayer too, just for me.

Then we hugged and kissed each other goodnight.

Eventually, Kevin began coming over for dates with Mom *and* me. I thought he seemed nice enough, and he appeared to make Mom laugh a lot. I guess Kevin could be pretty comical. If a character on the television was in a fight scene, Kevin mimicked the character as if he were in the action scene. Kevin threw punches at the air and made kickboxing moves as if he were engaged in a real martial arts fight. Mom and I thought he looked pretty silly, and we laughed out loud together.

Kevin's laugh was pretty funny too. If Kevin thought something was funny, you'd know it. He laughed so loud I was sure our neighbors could hear him. Mom would try to quiet him as she and I laughed at his enormous laughs, but Kevin didn't seem to care one bit about the loud sound coming out of him. He just laughed and laughed until the moment was done.

But one evening, Kevin was over for dinner, and he and mom were in a lively discussion about the president, and both of them began to raise their voices.

"Don't yell at my mom!" I interrupted.

"This is OUR house!" I said, slamming my fist on the dinner table.

Mom and Kevin were quite startled by my outburst, and they quickly explained that they were only having a debate, as adults sometimes do. But I needed to remind Kevin that he was just a guest, someone who visits for a while and then goes to their own home. And being mean to Mom was part of breaking the rules where we live.   Kevin told me how sorry he was for upsetting me.

I guess I never thought that it could be any other way. Kevin was just someone who takes Mom out on dates, and that hangs out with us sometimes.

I mean, what was a five-year-old to know about romantic love stuff.

CHAPTER THREE

Two Plus Three

Kevin had kids of his own, Sam and Becca.

Mom explained that Kevin had also gotten divorced from Becca and Sam's mom and that Becca and Sam lived with him, just like I lived with Mom after she and dad divorced.

Like my dad, Becca and Sam's mom lived several hours away. And like the schedule I had with my dad, Becca and Sam saw their mom some holidays or during spring break and every summer.

Dad visited me any extra chance he got. "I'll miss you," Mom would say with tears in her eyes as she kissed me goodbye and squeezed me one final time as she said goodbye to me at the start of summer break. I loved his piggyback rides, and dad let me eat scores of candies. But inevitably, I always missed home and missed Mom only after a couple of weeks.

Although Kevin seemed normal, I began to wonder if he was starving Becca and Sam. Becca and Sam never turned down a snack when they visited. They'd scarf it down and then ask for seconds. Mom must have seen my concern for the goldfish packs and apple sauce cups flying off the pantry shelves. "It's okay," she whispered. "I'll buy you more."

Becca and I danced on my musical mat, and Sam pushed me around in my toy car as he made traffic noises, and I beeped the horn. The three of usually only argued when it was time to agree on a place to eat. Becca loved pizza, Sam loved burgers, and I loved chicken nuggets. Mom and Kevin finally wised up and stopped asking the three of us what we wanted to eat or which restaurant we'd like to visit. Mom and Kevin decided, and if any of us were unhappy about their choice, they'd say, "There's always next time."

Any other arguments were usually between Becca and Sam. Becca, being the oldest, liked to be the boss of Sam. So, Becca and Sam fought when Sam wasn't doing something the way Becca thought it should be done.

While choosing popsicles during a trip to a waterpark, Becca insisted that Sam shouldn't get the lemon flavored one he'd selected because Becca knew he wouldn't like it.

"Sam, don't you remember?" Becca asked. "You had a lemon-flavored slushie at the amusement park last summer, and you hated it."

"So!" Sam responded.

"Then don't cry like a baby or complain if you don't like it!" Becca responded. "You should get the cotton candy-flavored popsicle that I'm getting. I think you'll like it better," Becca said.

"Becca, Sam can choose whichever flavor he wants," Kevin told her.

Maybe Becca was bossy because she was the only girl in their house. (And girls *are* smarter than boys).

Only two years later, Kevin and Mom would marry, and as much fun as Becca could bring to any situation, it turns out that she can be equally as bossy to *everyone*.

CHAPTER FOUR

The Truth Hurts

Mom jokes that she can recite every line and song in the movie *Tangled* because the two of us must have watched it at least once a week for an entire year when I was a preschooler. What little girl doesn't love a princess movie?

Rapunzel lived in a tower with her mom, Mother Gothel, who kept Rapunzel inside by telling her that the world outside was cruel and scary. Rapunzel's curiosity about the world beyond her tower grew as she got older. She eventually escapes from the tower and discovers that Mother Gothel isn't her mom, but instead an evil witch who had stolen Rapunzel when she was a baby so that she could have the power of Rapunzel's magical hair. At the end of the movie, Rapunzel is reunited with her real mom and dad, who hold Rapunzel in their arms as they cry tears of happiness. Then the entire kingdom celebrates the return of Princess Rapunzel.

Tangled is like most kid movies, I guess. There's always a happy ending.

"Why doesn't my dad live here?" I asked Mom once after the movie ended.

Mom said that although they loved each other, Mom and Dad thought they would get along better if they lived apart.

"But we both love you so much," she said as she stood from the sofa and headed into the kitchen.

After Mom told me that she would marry Kevin, I asked her again about her and my dad. I liked Kevin, but he wasn't my dad. Mom explained that Kevin could never take my dad's place, but instead, Kevin would be a second dad. A second dad to be there for me and help take care of me.

"You and dad can marry again, can't you?" I asked.

I was seven years old now. Mom paused as she usually does when she wants to explain adult stuff in a way that I can understand.

Why did Mom and Dad stop getting along? I thought. Did Kevin stop getting along with

Becca's and Sam's mom? What if Mom and Kevin stop getting along?

"Mia, your dad and I weren't getting along well, so we decided it was best we didn't remain married to each other. But we knew that we would always remain in each other's lives because we were committed to being your parents and providing you all the love that you deserve," she explained.

"Mom, did it have anything to do with me? Did I cause you guys not to get along?" I asked.

"No. Absolutely not. The truth is, honey, your dad and I started to have problems in our marriage well before you were born. We were young when we married, and when you are younger, you don't know nearly as much as you think you do. Your dad and I chose to marry, and that was not the right decision for us. But we tried for many years to make it work because we did love each other.

"Then God blessed us with you. You were so perfect, and we wanted nothing but the best for your life. We knew that you deserved the absolute best from us; you deserved two happy parents. Unfortunately, honey, your dad and I thought we could be happier, better parents by living apart."

Sometimes real life isn't like the kid movies.

Mom and dad aren't home, ready to give me a big hug at the end of each day. But unlike

Mother Gothel in *Tangled*, Mom told me the truth.

CHAPTER FIVE

Moving On

After the wedding, Mom and I moved from our apartment to live with Kevin, Becca, and Sam at their house.

Sure, I liked princess movies, but I was never into girly colors like pink or purple. Purple is Becca's favorite color, and now that I'm moving into her bedroom, it is now, sadly, my new wall color. On the brighter side, at least mom and Kevin decided that Becca and I shouldn't share a room, so Becca is moving into what used to be Kevin's office. I overhead Mom explaining to Kevin that she and my Aunt Sarah shared a room, and she felt punished for having to share a room with her little sister.

"Becca is fourteen years old," Mom continued. "Sure, Becca and Mia have common interests, but what teenager wants to share their space with a seven-year-old? I don't want Becca to feel that Mia and I are infringing on her territory any more than we already are."

Anyway, Becca's room was pretty messy. I think it's best that we kept my toys and her clothes in separate spaces.

Mom was right, though. Although Becca was a teenager, we actually shared a lot of things in common.

We both loved to draw and paint, but Becca was so much better at it than I was. Her sunsets were never simply an orange circle peeking out of a light blue sky. Instead, her sunsets were shades of orange, yellows, pinks, and blues. And she always uses crayons, pencils, and markers to outline and show different textures on the page. Becca never gave herself much credit for her pictures, saying she "couldn't draw at all." But I always thought she was really good at it.

The two of us continued our dance parties, and Becca would even let me do her hair and make-up, which always gave us a good laugh.

Becca was starting her freshman year of high school, but I'm not sure she liked it very much.

One day she came home from school upset, and I heard her say to Mom that she only had one good friend. "Well, Becca, that's all you need. A good friend. I'd certainly rather have one good friend than ten friends who I didn't like very much or get along with," Mom said.

"Besides," Mom continued, "as the year goes on, I'm sure you'll make more good friends."

When Becca's good friend Jennifer came to hang out, Becca would let me hang out with them. This was my big Sis Becca. I don't think Becca realized how cool she was. Sometimes, the three of us baked cookies or watched old Disney shows or movies that Becca and Jennifer watched when they were my age. I think Becca accepted me as the cute little sister she never knew she wanted.

But Jennifer had something that Becca and I both wanted. A dog. Becca loved animals too, just as much as I did, and we both wanted a dog for a pet. Mom had said once that maybe I could have a dog when I was older and could help take care of it.

Becca and Sam had a pet dog once, but it wasn't very nice to Sam when he was born, so Kevin had to find their dog a new home. Becca had always hoped for another one. Maybe together, Becca and I could convince Mom and Kevin it was time for a new family pet.

CHAPTER SIX

Competition

"Come on, Sam! You got this!" Kevin yelled. Sam had just taken possession of the ball on the rebound and was speeding up the court. He'd already scored seven points in the first half, and in less than a minute into the third quarter, it looked like he'd score again. "He swooshed it!" Mom yelled. And just like that, Sam had put three more points on the board for the Mustangs.

Kevin had signed Sam up for a neighborhood basketball league. I heard Kevin tell Mom that he thought it would be great for Sam to learn sportsmanship and build more camaraderie with other ten-year-old boys.

"What's camaraderie?" Sam asked Kevin on our way home from school one afternoon.

"It means you'll have the chance to make more friendships with the players on your team," Kevin explained. Sam seemed indifferent to trying basketball.

"Besides Sam," Kevin continued. "You're pretty tall for your age. You'll probably be a natural at basketball," he said.

I have to admit that Sam was pretty good. I mean, this was just the third game of the season, and he had been the top scorer of his team in both of the previous games. Sam seemed to like the extra attention too. "Did you see how high I jumped when I rebounded the ball?" Sam would ask us on the car ride home. Or "Did you see how I dribbled the ball between my legs?" he asked.

I also have to admit that I didn't like the extra attention Sam was getting from playing basketball, including screams from Mom during the game and high-fives to Sam at the end of another great game.

Mom was MY cheerleader at every swim practice. Mom screamed for me alone at every ballet recital. Our walks were *our* walks—just the two of us. Mom watched *me* climb the monkey bars at the park. Mom watched *me* ride my bike. Just *me*. Now when I played outside, it was usually me, Mom, *and* Sam.

"Dawn, look! Watch me do this cool skateboard trick," Sam would say to Mom.

"Cool trick, Sam," Mom would yell.

"Mia, look! Can you do this?" Sam asked as he flipped the skateboard over with his foot and jumped on.

Sam is such a showoff, I thought to myself. First of all, I'm only seven. Second of all, I have never owned a skateboard. So no, Sam. I can't do that!

"Do you love Sam more than you love me?" I asked Mom as she tucked me into bed one night.

"Of course not, Mia. Why would you ask such a thing, sweetheart?"

"Because you cheer Sam on, tell him how good he does, and… and… you tell him you love him when you tuck him into bed too."

"Mia," Mom started. "I will always love you, and there is nothing that could ever change that. But honey, just as you were God's gift to me, God has now blessed me with three more beautiful gifts, Kevin, Becca, and Sam, and I will love and cherish Kevin, Becca, and Sam just as I cherish you. And I pray that one day, you will love and cherish them too."

When Sam wasn't a showoff, the two of us got along pretty well. Our bedrooms are right across the hall from each other, and I'd begun to learn a lot from my new big brother. The only lego toy

I ever owned was a Disney princess lego set I'd gotten for my 3rd birthday.

Sam had a humongous 18-gallon tote full of lego bricks. Not just pink and purple lego bricks, but lego bricks of all sorts of colors. Apparently, some of these were original lego bricks that Kevin had as a kid. I learned to build homes, cars, planes, and superheroes, all alongside my new big brother. Sam and I could play with lego bricks for hours.

Sam also loved video games and had just gotten his very own computer for his room before we moved in. Sam invited me to pull up a chair and watch him play. Again- Sam likes attention.

I must admit I liked the attention too. I liked being invited into my big bro's room. It made me feel cool.

Sam was pretty popular in school, at least with the girls. Over dinner, he once told us that a girl slipped him a note during recess. And once, while attending a classmate's birthday party, Sam came home upset because a group of girls followed him around the trampoline park the entire time while he just wanted to have fun with his friends.

But Sam seemed to make new friends wherever we went. Soon after arriving at the neighborhood pool once, Sam joined in a diving game with two other boys and swam with them the entire time we were there. He'd only met them that afternoon at the pool for the very first time.

That was Sam. Athletic, apparently cute to *some* girls, and a friend to anyone.

CHAPTER SEVEN

Quiet Time

Spring Break was almost here, and it was time for our first official family vacation. Mom and Kevin held a family meeting so that each of us could give some input as to where we would like to travel.

"The beach!" Becca shouted.

"Which beach?" Kevin asked.

"Any beach," Becca said.

Sam suggested California so that he could see the house of one of his favorite you tubers.

"What about you, Mia?" Mom asked.

I suggested that we visit Africa to tour a safari. Becca and Sam laughed at me.

"Stop it, now," Kevin directed to Becca and Sam.

Mom said that a trip to Africa wasn't quite doable since we were only out of school for one week. Then she walked over to the bookshelf to grab the globe.

Oh no, I thought, another one of Mom's "teachable moments," as she likes to call them.

"So, honey," she started, "Please find where we are located currently."

"Mom... I know. We live in one of the fifty states of the United States of America, which is located on the continent of North America," I answered begrudgingly.

"We are here," I said, pointing to Texas, and then followed our state's southern border with my finger, tracing the shape of a cowboy boot.

"Great," Mom said. "Now find Africa."

"Africa is here I said, turning the globe. We will head east and cross the Atlantic Ocean."

"Right." Mom said.

"And Africa is another one of the seven continents!" shouted Sam."

"Right again." Mom said.

"Travel by car isn't reasonable, but we could reach Africa by plane," Mom said.

"Any idea how long the flight would be?" she asked.

"No," I said.

"At least eight hours!" Becca chimed in.

"Becca, it's at least double that amount of time," Mom said, "but good guess."

"Any idea which country you'd like to visit?" Mom asked.

"Well, Mrs. Taylor, the librarian, read us a story a few weeks ago about endangered lions in West Africa," I said. "So, I don't know, maybe Nigeria," I said, scanning the continent.

"Or, what about this city?" Sammy asked, pointing to Senegal (pronounced Sin – a – gaul).

"Sam, Senegal, is a country rather than a city, Mom explained. "The country of Senegal has its own cities."

Mom and Kevin agreed that a trip to a country in Africa would be an incredible vacation someday, just not this time around.

We ultimately settled on Florida. It had the beaches Becca wanted, the sun of California, and an aquarium and a large zoo for me. Kevin's parents, my extra grandparents, live there too. It was a win for everyone.

Once we arrived in Ft. Myers, Mom told Grandma Susan that navigating the airport and boarding a plane had never been so chaotic.

Grandma Susan laughed as she gave Mom a big hug.

Mom handed all of us our boarding passes as we stood in line to go through security and have our carry-on bags scanned. Becca misplaced her boarding pass while we waited, and we had to let several other passengers go ahead of us until she found it. As we started to board the plane, Mom told everyone to look at their boarding pass to see their assigned seat number.

"Ughhhh, I'm next to Becca," Sam complained. "I want to sit next to dad."

"I don't want to sit next to you either. I want to sit next to Mia," Becca said to Sam.

"I want to sit next to Mom," I said.

"Mia, you're next to Becca and Sam," Mom replied.

"But I want to sit next to you," I said.

"I want to sit next to your mom," Kevin chimed in.

"Listen," Mom said. "We placed you kids in three seats together."

"Your dad and I would like to have some adult time," Mom said to Sam and me.

"But Becca and I will fight," Sam said.

Mom took a look at all of the other passengers behind us in line, also heading to their seats, and shot Kevin an exasperated look.

"Okay, girls will sit together on this side," Mom said, pointing to three seats on the left side of the plane on Row 23. "Kevin, you and Sam take the two seats together on the right side of the plane."

"I want the window," I called.

"I want the window seat too," Becca retorted.

"I'm sitting on the aisle. Figure it out you two," Mom told us sternly.

"And to all of you," Mom continued while eyeing the four of us. "I want twenty minutes of quiet time as soon as this plane taxis from the gate."

Quiet time is Mom's way of saying that she has had enough for now, and don't bother her until she regains some patience to deal with you.

Mom told my kindergarten teacher once that I was a rule follower. I had an easy-going personality, a little shy with new people, but I liked to follow the rules. Mom was right. Generally, I do as I'm told, mainly because I don't want Mom, or my teachers for that matter, upset with me. I hated to see the disappointment in Mom's eyes or hear how upset she was with me in her voice.

Becca and I settled on me getting the window seat. Sometimes being the youngest kid works to my advantage. Becca only wanted to use the window for a headrest in case she tried to sleep. On the other hand, I argued that I would like to use the window to see things outside of the window, such as the view of the sky above the clouds or the view of the world thousands of feet below us. From up high, the world and everything in it seem so tiny. I can't help but think of *Alice in Wonderland* when Alice drinks the potion and shrinks to what appears the size of a pea compared to everything else in the room before she uses the key to fit through the tiny door into the beautiful garden. Everything below us would be the perfect size for Alice.

So off we went in silence, for the next twenty minutes anyway.

CHAPTER EIGHT

Conflict

"I wish you were still married to my dad!" I cried as Mom tried to console me. "Why did you and Dad have to get a divorce?"

"Honey calm down, and tell me what happened," Mom said.

"While you were gone, Kevin yelled at me. All I did was ride my bike across a small part of the grass near the sidewalk! It was an accident! I told him it was an accident. He said that he'd just put chemicals on that part of the grass to help it grow. I said sorry, but I could tell he was still mad at me. And Sam butted in and told Kevin that it wasn't an accident. Sam is so annoying! I screamed.

"And Kevin cares about grass more than me! I don't want to live here anymore!" I cried.

Mom just let me sob in her arms for a few minutes.

"Honey, you know that Kevin cares for you more than he does the grass. I do not doubt how much he loves you. I would not have married Kevin if I didn't believe with all of my heart that he loves you just as much as he loves me, Becca, and Sam.

"And Mia, I also know that Kevin has since apologized to you for yelling. He knows that he hurt your feelings by yelling. Kevin is your parent now too, and parents are not perfect, honey. We make mistakes too, even when it involves our kids. Haven't I had to apologize to you when I didn't handle something very well?" Mom asked.

"Yeah," I shrugged.

"Baby," Mom continued, "I'm married to Kevin now. Your dad and I are not going to be married again. And although there may be times that Kevin and I may become upset with one another, we have committed to being together as a family, no matter what. Kevin, Becca, and Sam are a part of our family now. And just as Kevin and I may become upset with one another, you and Becca and Sam may become upset with each other too. But it doesn't mean that we should not be a family.

"And by the way, your Uncle Bo was SO annoying to me too sometimes. I think big brothers just like to annoy their little sisters," Mom said while giving me a smile and a nudge.

I was too young to remember what it was like when Mom and Dad were married. The truth is, I don't know what my life would have been like had Mom and Dad stayed married. I imagine it would have been pretty perfect, just the three of us- for me anyway. I mean, Dad and I have so much fun together. I imagine we'd have loads more fun if I could see him every day. And I wouldn't have to share Mom with anyone. She'd be there only for me.

But Mom said they weren't happy together, and I know Mom is happy now. Dad also seems happy. And I'm pretty happy too. I know Kevin loves me, and I love him. That's why it hurt my feelings so bad when he got upset with me. I love Becca and Sam too, even after we disagree or fight.

CHAPTER NINE

Family of Six

"Water bottles?" Mom asked.

"Check."

"Sunscreen?"

"Check."

"Bug repellant?"

"Check."

"Leash?"

Check.

Mom and Kevin were making the usual check-off list in the front of the car as we all piled into the backseat before leaving home.

We headed out for a hike at a nearby park—one of our favorite things to do.

"Come on, Rex, hop up, boy!" Sam said.

Our new golden retriever, Rex, settled into my lap for the quick car ride. Car rides made Rex a little nervous, but it helped to let him stick his head out of the window for a bit.

"I want to hold him on the way home, okay," Becca says to me.

Mom and Kevin surprised us with a new puppy, Rex, just after my ninth birthday. Mom said that she thought all of us kids could pitch in to help take care of him.

Rex is almost a year old now, and he is the best dog ever. He loves to play tug a war, and I have even taught him a few tricks.

Becca and I screamed and hugged each other in excitement when we first saw Rex. I think Sam was in total shock. He just stood there, eyes wide, repeating, "Is he really ours?"

"Everyone out," Kevin announced as he placed the car in park.

"Who wants the leash?" Mom asked.

"Me," Sam said.

"Thanks, Mia," Sam said while I held Rex tight so Sam could get his leash on.

"Mia, come on," Kevin said. "You and I will lead the way," he said as he reached for my hand.

"Come on, guys!" I shouted, running ahead to catch up.

My family may not be the one I once hoped for—one with me, Mom, and Dad. But it's what I have. It's been nearly three years since Mom and Kevin married, and although we may have our disagreements sometimes, Becca, Sam, and I have a lot of fun together. I mean, if it had just been Mom and me, I'm not sure I would have as much fun. Becca and I soaked each other with the water hose just the other day, and without Sam, who would I have nerf gun battles with?

I've learned a lot from Kevin too. Although Dad got me to ride my first bike without the training wheels, Kevin was there to teach me how to ride my new bigger bike when Mom was too afraid to let go of my seat. "Dawn, she can do it, he said. She's a big girl. Mia can handle it."

Kevin has taught me a lot about gardening too. I've helped him plant a few flowers and vegetables in our garden. Kevin often reminds Mom of the dead plants he saw on our patio when he and Mom started dating. Mom admits that she should have chosen plants that didn't need to be watered each day.

Kevin and I stopped for a water break almost a mile into the hike, giving the rest of the gang a chance to catch up.

"How are the two guides doing?" Mom panted as she caught up with Kevin and me.

Kevin pulled Mom in for a big hug and kiss.

"Ewwww!"

"Gross!"

"No, stop!" All of us kids yell.

"I love you," he says to Mom with a big smile.

"I love all of you!" Kevin says as he pulls me in for a hug.

Mom, Kevin, Becca, Sam, and Me. This is our family.

Wait! Let's try that again.

Mom, Kevin, Becca, Sam, Me, *and* Rex. This is our family. My happily ever after.

Printed in Great Britain
by Amazon